MY BACK YARD

Anne & Harlow Rockwell

MACMILLAN PUBLISHING COMPANY NEW YORK

Macmillan Publishing Company
866 Third Avenue, New York, N.Y. 10022
Collier Macmillan Canada, Inc.

Printed in the United States of America

10   9   8   7   6   5   4   3   2   1

Library of Congress Cataloging in Publication Data
Rockwell, Anne F.
My back yard.
(My world)
Summary: A little girl finds many things to do and
enjoy in her back yard.
[1. Gardens—Fiction]   I. Rockwell, Harlow.
II. Title.   III. Series.
PZ7.R5943Mv 1984   [E]   83-18717
ISBN 0-02-777690-5

Do you know where I go
when I go out the kitchen door?

This is where I go.
This is my own back yard.
It has a fence around it
with a gate
that opens and shuts.

This is the big maple tree
that grows in my back yard.

I can climb the little apple tree
all by myself.

This is the rosebush
where the bees come to buzz.

This is the birdbath
where the birds wash their feathers.

This is the bird feeder
where they eat their seeds.

And up in the maple tree there is a nest
where a family of blue jays lives.
Squirrels jump through the branches
and run up and down the trunk.

There is a clothesline in my back yard
where the clean clothes fly in the breeze
and dry in the sun.

I like to run in and out
among the drying clothes.
Sometimes I pretend they are chasing me.
Sometimes I pretend I am chasing them.
That is fun.

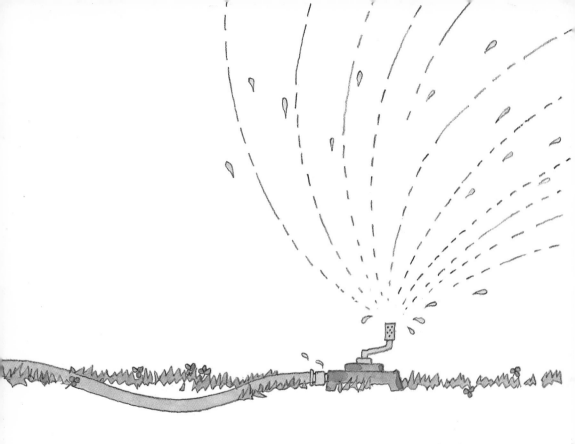

There is a sprinkler on the garden hose
to water the lawn.
I wear my bathing suit to play in the sprinkler.

I run and jump through the spray.
It makes me feel wet and cool
in the hot sun.

Green grass grows
in my back yard.
I like to lie on it
and look up at the clouds.

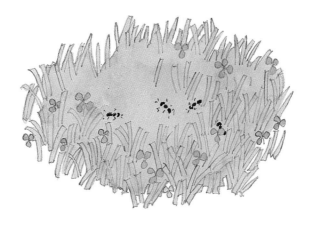

Then I roll over and hunt for
four-leaf clovers.
I like to watch the little ants
come and go through the green grass.

This is my sandbox
where I build with my shovel and pail.
My father made my sandbox.

This is my swing.

Our neighbor's cat likes to climb
over the fence to visit me.
She likes to sit in the shade

under our picnic table.
She doesn't chase my birds.
She just stays quietly and blinks her eyes
and watches me play.
She is a good cat, I think.

I come indoors from my back yard
when it is time for lunch.

But then I go outside to play some more.
I like my back yard.